MW00886311

This
Treasure Cove Story
belongs to

_____

PET TALENT SHOW!

A CENTUM BOOK 978-1-910114-72-8
Published in Great Britain by Centum Books Ltd.
This edition published 2020.

1 3 5 7 9 10 8 6 4 2

Centum Books Ltd, 20 Devon Square, Newton Abbot,
Devon, TQ12 2HR, UK.

www.centumbooksltd.co.uk | books@centumbooksltd.co.uk
CENTUM BOOKS Limited Reg. No. 07641486.

A CIP catalogue record for this book is available
from the British Library.

Printed in China.

centum

A Treasure Cove Story

SHIMMER & SHINE

Pet Talent Show!

Adapted by Mickie Matheis
Based on the teleplay 'Untamed Talent' by Dustin Ferrer
Illustrated by Cartobaleno

It was an exciting day in Zahramay Falls – the amazing Pet Talent Show was just about to start!

Shimmer, Shine and Leah peeked out from behind the curtain. They couldn't wait to watch their furry friends perform. Plus, the winning pet would get one wish granted by Princess Samira herself!

A few minutes later, Zeta watched her pet dragon, Nazboo, practise his dance moves. As usual, the tricky sorceress was up to no good!

'When we win, you're going to wish for a gem that will make me the most powerful person in Zahramay Falls!' Zeta reminded her pet.

The little dragon nodded and went back to dancing.

It was showtime! The first pet to perform
was Leah's fox, Parisa. Using her tail and paws,
Parisa painted a magical masterpiece… and then
disappeared into it!

Princess Samira and the genie audience cheered.
They loved it!

Zeta was worried. 'That act was better than
I thought it would be.' She gave Nazboo a grin.
'Come on. Let's go cheat!'

Next up was Shine's pet tiger, Nahal.
'Nahal is going to play a tiger tune on her keyboard!' Shine announced. The genie snapped her fingers, and a giant keyboard appeared. 'Go get 'em, tiger!'

Nahal pounced on the keys and played 'Mary had a little lamb.'

'This act is good, too,' Zeta said. 'There must
be something I can do to ruin it.'
Nazboo stood nearby, playing with a feather.
That gave Zeta an idea. She cast a spell on the
feather and sent it floating out onstage to distract
the tiger cub.

Sure enough, Nahal spotted the feather and started to chase it! She raced up and down the giant keyboard, swatting at the floating feather.

But things didn't go quite the way Zeta had hoped. With every step Nahal took, her song sounded better and better. The crowd applauded wildly!

'Ugh! I can't believe my plan backfired!' Zeta moaned. 'If we want to win this contest, we have to make sure the next act is terrible!'

It was time for Shimmer's pet monkey, Tala, to perform.

'She's going to do a super-super-super-cute dance,' Shimmer told the audience.

Zeta was outraged. 'They're doing a dance? But *we're* doing a dance! Those genies have gone too far!'

'Let's see if that monkey can dance on slippery ice,' the sneaky sorceress muttered. 'Slide and slip, fall and spin. Turn to ice so we can win!' she chanted.

Suddenly, the stage floor turned into a sheet of ice!

But instead of falling, Tala began to glide and leap like a graceful ice-skater. Her final move was to carve a silly monkey face into the ice!

The audience was amazed! And another one of Zeta's plans had backfired.

Just then, Nazboo's name was called. It was Zeta's
pet's turn to perform!

Zeta had to think fast. Maybe Nazboo could still
win if his act had some extra-special flair. Zeta quickly
cast a spell on the props in the dressing room.

She held her breath as Nazboo began. The dragon's
first steps were perfect – until one of the enchanted
props flew across the stage!

Nazboo wobbled and tripped as the enchanted props tumbled around the theatre. Curtains ripped. Lights fell. Pillars tipped over. Pets ran from the runaway props. It was chaos!

Nazboo acted fast! Using a curtain cord, the little dragon swung around and saved all the other pets from the flying props. He delivered each pet safely to its owner.

Then he ran towards Princess Samira. A giant pillar was about
to topple over onto the princess and her pet peacock, Roya!
    Nazboo pushed their seats out of the way just as the entire
set came crashing down.
    Nazboo had saved the princess and the peacock!

Zeta stepped onto the stage and looked apologetically at the audience. 'Sorry about the mess,' she said sadly. She picked up Nazboo and was just about to leave when Princess Samira appeared in a poof of sparkles.

'Hold on, Zeta,' the princess said sweetly. 'I have to announce the winner.'

'Roya and I thought all the acts were Zahramazing!'
the princess said to the audience. 'But there was one
performer who was talented *and* brave. The winner
of the Pet Talent Show is… Nazboo!'
The genies and their pets clapped and cheered.

Zeta tried not to look surprised. 'Well, of
course I knew Nazboo would win,' she said.
'For his prize, he would like to wish for a gem.'
    'And which one would you like?' the princess
asked Nazboo.
    The dragon whispered into her ear.

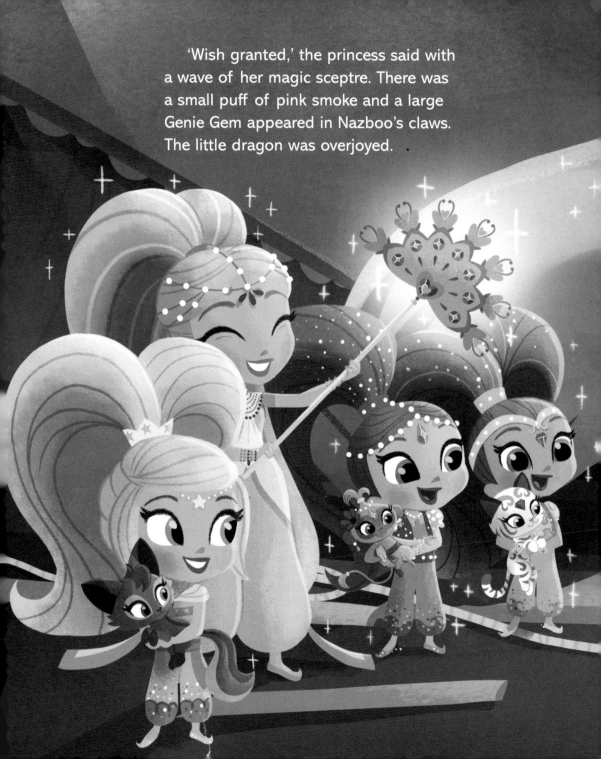

'Wish granted,' the princess said with
a wave of her magic sceptre. There was
a small puff of pink smoke and a large
Genie Gem appeared in Nazboo's claws.
The little dragon was overjoyed.

Zeta immediately snatched it from him. 'Finally! This gem will make me the most powerful person in Zahramay Falls!'

She cackled gleefully and hugged the gem
close. To her surprise, it let out a loud squeak!
Zeta stared at the gem, confused.

She glared at her pet. 'Nazboo, did you wish for a squeaky-toy gem?'

Nazboo nodded.

Zeta groaned. 'All that work for a squeaky toy!'

But the other pets thought Nazboo's pick was just perfect.

Thanks to Nazboo, the Pet Talent Show ended with a bang – and a squeak!

Treasure Cove Stories

Please contact Centum Books to receive the full list of titles in the *Treasure Cove Stories* series.
books@centumbooksltd.co.uk

Classic favourites

1 Three Little Pigs
2 Snow White and the Seven Dwarfs
3 The Fox and the Hound - Hide-and-Seek
4 Dumbo
5 Cinderella
6 Cinderella's Friends
7 Alice in Wonderland
8 Mad Hatter's Tea Party from Alice in Wonderland
9 Mickey Mouse and his Spaceship
10 Peter Pan
11 Pinocchio
12 Mickey and the Beanstalk
13 Sleeping Beauty and the Good Fairies
14 The Lucky Puppy
15 Chicken Little
16 The Incredibles
17 Coco
18 Winnie the Pooh and Tigger
19 The Sword in the Stone
20 Mary Poppins
21 The Jungle Book
22 The Aristocats
23 Lady and the Tramp
24 Bambi
25 Bambi - Friends of the Forest

Recently published

50 Frozen
51 Cinderella is my Babysitter
52 Beauty and the Beast - I am the Beast
53 Blaze and the Monster Machines - Mighty Monster Machines
54 Blaze and the Monster Machines - Dino Parade!
55 Teenage Mutant Ninja Turtles - Follow the Ninja!

56 I am a Princess
57 The Big Book of Paw Patrol
58 Paw Patrol - Adventures with Grandpa!
59 Paw Patrol - Pirate Pups!
60 Trolls
61 Trolls Holiday
62 The Secret Life of Pets
63 Zootropolis
64 Ariel is my Babysitter
65 Tiana is my Babysitter
66 Belle is my Babysitter
67 Paw Patrol - Itty-Bitty Kitty Rescue
68 Moana
69 Nella the Princess Knight - My Heart is Bright!
70 Guardians of the Galaxy
71 Captain America - High-Stakes Heist!
72 Ant-Man
73 The Mighty Avengers
74 The Mighty Avengers - Lights Out!
75 The Incredible Hulk
76 Shimmer & Shine - Wish Upon a Sleepover
77 Shimmer & Shine - Backyard Ballet
78 Paw Patrol - All-Star Pups!
79 Teenage Mutant Ninja Turtles - Really Spaced Out!
80 I am Ariel
81 Madagascar
82 Jasmine is my Babysitter
83 How to Train your Dragon
84 Shrek
85 Puss in Boots
86 Kung Fu Panda
87 Beauty and the Beast - I am Belle
88 The Lion Guard - The Imaginary Okapi
89 Thor - Thunder Strike!
90 Guardians of the Galaxy - Rocket to the Rescue!
91 Nella the Princess Knight - Nella and the Dragon
92 Shimmer & Shine - Treasure Twins!

93 Olaf's Frozen Adventure
94 Black Panther
95 Trolls - Branch's Bunker Birthday
96 Trolls - Poppy's Party
97 The Ugly Duckling
98 Cars - Look Out for Mater!
99 101 Dalmatians
100 The Sorcerer's Apprentice
101 Tangled
102 Avengers - The Threat of Thanos
103 Puppy Dog Pals - Don't Rain on my Pug-Rade
104 Jurassic Park
105 The Mighty Thor
106 Doctor Strange

Latest publications

107 Captain Marvel
108 The Invincible Iron Man
109 Black Panther - Warriors of Wakanda
110 The Big Freeze
111 Ratatouille
112 Aladdin
113 Aladdin - I am the Genie
114 Seven Dwarfs Find a House
115 Toy Story
116 Toy Story 4
117 Paw Patrol - Jurassic Bark!
118 Paw Patrol - Mighty Pup Power!
119 Shimmer & Shine - Pet Talent Show!
120 SpongeBob SquarePants - Krabby Patty Caper
121 The Lion King - I am Simba
122 Winnie the Pooh - The Honey Tree
123 Frozen II
124 Baby Shark and the Colours of the Ocean
125 Baby Shark and the Police Sharks!
126 Trolls World Tour

*Book list may be subject to change.